Penguin Pandemonium
The Rescue

Penguin Pandemonium

The Rescue

Jeanne Willis

Illustrated by Nathan Reed

BARRON'S

First edition for the United States published
in 2013 by Barron's Educational Series, Inc.

Text © 2012 Jeanne Willis
Inside illustrations © 2012 Nathan Reed
Cover illustration © 2012 Ed Vere

First published in 2012 by HarperCollins Children's Books
77-85 Fulham Palace Road
Hammersmith, London W6 8JB

All inquiries should be addressed to:
Barron's Educational Series, Inc.
250 Wireless Boulevard
Hauppauge, New York 11788
www.barronseduc.com

ISBN: 978-1-4380-0306-1

Library of Congress Catalog No.: 2013936282

Date of Manufacture: July 2013
Manufactured by: B12V12G, Berryville, VA

Printed in the United States of America
9 8 7 6 5 4 3 2 1

Meet the Penguins!

Rory, Eddie, & Clive

Rockhopper

Looks: Rockhoppers have spiky yellow and black feathers on their heads that look like long eyebrows.

How big? 18 to 23 inches—about half the size of adult Emperor Penguins.

Favorite food: Shrimp.

Penguin party trick: Rockhopper Penguins love to burst from the water and land on the rocks with a belly flop.

Flipper fact: They hop from rock to rock, keeping both feet together and can jump up to five feet.

FAIRY

Little Blue, Muriel, Hatty, & Brenda

Looks: Fairy Penguins have blue feathers on their heads and backs but have white bellies.

How big? 12 to 13 inches—the world's smallest penguin.

Favorite food: Sardines and anchovies.

Penguin party trick: In the wild, Fairy Penguins are nocturnal so they only go on land at night (well past the Rockhoppers' bedtime).

Flipper fact: The world's smallest penguin—they are also known as the Little Penguin, or the Little Blue Penguin.

EMPEROR

Paulie, Alaskadabra, Teeny, & Tiny (chicks)

Looks: Emperor Penguins have black backs, white tummies, and bright splashes of yellow and orange on their front and their ears. The chicks are fluffy and gray and their faces are white, not black.

How big?! Up to three feet tall—the world's tallest and heaviest penguin (over three times as tall as Little Blue!).

Favorite food: Squid.

Penguin party trick: When an egg is laid, the male stands with the egg on his feet to keep it warm until it hatches (this can take up to nine weeks).

Flipper fact: Emperor Penguins can stay under water for nearly twenty minutes!

CHINSTRAP

Waldo, Warren, and Wesley

Looks: Chinstrap Penguins get their name from the small black band that runs under their chin.

How big? Up to 27 inches (twice as tall as Fairy Penguins).

Favorite food: Little shrimp called krill.

Penguin party trick: Chinstraps are also known as Stonecracker Penguins because their call is so harsh it sounds like it could break stones.

Flipper fact: Chinstraps are the most common type of penguin—there are about thirteen million of them in the world.

THE Famous
FLYING PENGUIN...

Flighty Almighty

… Ahem, he's a GOOSE!

CHAPTER ONE

Bad Chicks

It was perfect weather for penguins. It had snowed heavily in the night and the penguin enclosure at City Zoo looked just like the Arctic. The wooden huts where they slept glittered under a frosty duvet like a row of mini igloos and there were

icicles hanging off the palace where Big Paulie the emperor penguin lived.

It was so cold, the penguin pool had frozen and to Rory the rockhopper's delight, the

ice was thick enough to stand on. He tested it carefully with one foot, then both feet—it seemed perfectly safe—but the two bears who were watching him had their doubts.

"You're skating on thin ice, matey!" shouted Orson.

"Don't come crying to us when it cracks and you freeze your tail off," added Ursie.

Rory looked up at them, but instead of the two brown bears that normally lived in the paddock, there appeared to be two polar bears.

"Ugh! I hate the way the flakes stick to my fur when I make a snow angel," said Orson, brushing himself down and revealing his true colors.

"Some angel," grunted Ursie. "You're the Nightbear before Christmas."

Just then, Blue the little fairy penguin came skidding over.

"Hey, Rory! What are you waiting for?" she laughed, grabbing his flipper and dragging him onto the ice. "I can't remember the last time the pool froze."

"Nor can I," said Rory, spinning her around. "It must have been when we were eggs."

"It was way before that," said Ursie. "It was in 2008 on a Tuesday. I remember it well because a tubby, old emperor penguin didn't realize it was thawing, and fell through in a very comical manner."

"That was Alaskadabra," said Orson. "He had to be rescued by that boss of yours."

"Yeah, Big Paulie," chortled Ursie. "I've never seen anything so funny in all my life."

"Hey, who are you calling funny?" barked a gruff voice from the edge of the pool. "Show some respect or I'll have my good friend Mister Tiger turn you into a rug."

It was Paulie. He looked even bigger and even more fierce than usual to Rory. Even the bears backed off, but the two

fluffy emperor chicks hanging on to his tail weren't the slightest bit scared of him.

"Thwing me with your flipperth, Uncky Pooey!" lisped Teeny, poking the mighty emperor in the tummy.

"No, let'th play thkidding!" insisted Tiny, folding his relative in half by buckling him behind the knees.

Big Paulie might have been in charge of the grown-up penguins—he'd had years of practice—but taking care of two frisky toddlers was a very different task. He cleared his throat and beckoned to Rory.

"I think he wants to talk to you," said Blue.

"Me?" muttered Rory.

"Yes, you!" boomed Paulie.

Rory skated over to the edge of the pool and hopped out. The boss stared at him with his beady eyes while the twin chicks made funny faces and poked out their tiny tongues.

"Listen, Rory. I have some very urgent business to attend to."

"No, he doethn't!" giggled Teeny.

Big Paulie took a deep breath and continued.

"Yes, I do and I'm already late for... my... meeting about... stuff."

"Uncky Pooey, you're telling fibth!" said Tiny, smacking him hard on the back. "Mommy paid you two big mackerelth to look after uth and you thaid you wathn't bithy!"

Paulie threw his flippers in the air.

"Rory, the fact of the matter is, I have to be elsewhere," he said. Then his voice broke. "And as your boss, I'm *begging* you to babysit!"

"But I've never looked after chicks before," said Rory, dreading the prospect and looking to Blue for backup.

"He'll be terrible at it," said Blue.

Big Paulie shrugged.

"Oh, please. How hard can it be, Rory? I'm not asking for much—simply that you swear to keep my beloved nephew and niece safe from harm. I'm putting all my trust in you."

Before Rory could answer, Paulie shook the twins off his legs and, leaving them fooling around in the snow, waddled off, calling back over his shoulder.

"And I mustn't be disturbed until this evening!"

Rory sighed. If Big Paulie said something had to be done, it had to be done, but it wasn't going to be easy looking after the chicks. In fact, they seemed determined to make it as hard as possible and kept toddling off in opposite directions.

"Come back!" he insisted, "I need you in one place to babysit you."

"No, Wory!" stamped Teeny. "Uth ith too old for you to thit on!"

"You will thquash uth!" said Tiny as Rory ran after him. "Chathe me, Wory!"

Blue smiled to herself. Rory was usually so fast on the ice that he could perform the best stunts, but at the moment he was going cross-eyed trying to get the chicks under control.

"Help me, Blue!" he pleaded as Teeny sat on him and Tiny rubbed snow in his head feathers.

"I thought you'd never ask," she grinned. "Right, you two! Who wants a story?"

"Oooh, *uth* wanth a thtory!" they squealed.

Abandoning Rory, they waddled over to Blue and cuddled up.

"Are you sitting comfortably?" she asked.

"No. We want Wory to thit nexth to uth too," said Teeny. "Group hugth!"

Blue patted the rock next to her, Rory sat down and they all snuggled up.

"Kith me, Wory," said Tiny. "Mommy alwayth kithith uth before a thtory."

Rory shifted uncomfortably.

"You can have a kiss at the end, but only if you're good," said Blue.

Then she began. "Once upon a time, there were two naughty chicks…"

She had just got their attention when Muriel and her girly gang of fairy penguins arrived. Seeing this cozy scene, Muriel felt it was her solemn duty to embarrass Blue and Rory as much as possible.

"Oh my cod! Bloop and Rory are playing mommies and daddies."

Blue blushed and held up her beak.

"No, we are not! We're babysitting for Paulie."

Muriel preened her chest and snorted.

"Yeah, right. Hatty and Brenda, don't you think Bloop and Rory are so like an old married couple?"

Secretly, Hatty and Brenda were jealous of Blue cuddled up to Rory with the cute chicks, but they didn't dare admit it in front of their leader.

"So married," said Hatty.

"So old couple," added Brenda.

Rory was just going to shout, "So what?" when his best friends Eddie and

Clive came roaring by on their new snowboards. Worried that he looked sappy sitting there, he leapt to his feet.

"Snow's up, dude!" whooped Clive.

Rory jumped onto the back of Eddie's board.

"I'm on it already. Let's go!"

Blue's beak fell open.

"Rory! Don't you dare leave me with the kids—"

But he was gone. Muriel tilted her head to the side and blinked at her.

"Bloop, you are *so* second-best," she simpered.

Normally, Blue would have stood up to Muriel, but she didn't want to move because the chicks had just fallen asleep.

The last thing she wanted to do was wake them, so she put her head in the air and looked the other way.

"What are you doing—looking for a new boyfriend?" persisted Muriel. "Face it, Bloop, Rory doesn't want to play happy families with you, does he, Hatty and Brenda?"

Hatty and Brenda were so smitten with the chicks they were hardly paying attention.

"Happy," murmured Hatty.

"Families," sighed Brenda.

Muriel flicked their beaks.

"Don't go all sappy on me! Come along, girls. Let's go and make a Snow-Muriel. I feel like posing... Bloop, you'd better stay there in case Rory comes back... like... *never!*"

But Rory did come back. As soon as he'd gone, he'd had second thoughts about it and managed to persuade his friends to let Blue join in. "Blue's like one of the guys," he insisted. "We can do better stunts with all four of us." They shook their heads no, so he had to come up with another tactic.

"I'll give you two squid at feeding time," said Rory reluctantly.

"Four squid," said Clive. "Half for me, half for Eddie."

"I'd rather have a whole one," said Eddie.

The deal was done and Rory went back to fetch Blue, hoping that she would let him have some of her squid later.

"You took your time," she said.

He held out his flippers apologetically.

"That's Eddie and Clive for you. They never take no for an answer."

Teeny and Tiny had fallen into a deep sleep and were huddled up so tightly that they looked like one big chick with four eyes.

"Come and play while they're sleeping," suggested Rory. "We might not get snow as good as this again for years."

Blue checked on the chicks, who showed no sign of waking.

"OK, but not for long—and not too far away."

"They'll be fine," said Rory.

Blue believed him and they hurried off together to join the boys, filled with excitement at the thought of snowboarding down the ice.

Blue wasn't disappointed. The speed she reached as she raced down the slide almost took her breath away. Even Clive and Eddie were impressed.

"World speed record or what, Blue!" cheered Rory. "Right, let's see if I can beat you."

"Shouldn't we get back to the chicks?" she asked.

But this was the best snow ever; it would be a crime to waste it.

"Just one more turn," said Rory.

But he had two more turns. Then three.

Blue didn't stop him—she didn't want him to think she was a spoilsport.

By the time they got back, however, the chicks were gone.

CHAPTER TWO

Chick-napped!

Rory and Blue stared at the spot where they had left Teeny and Tiny sleeping, but all that remained of them was a shallow dip where the warmth of their bodies had melted the ice. If the chicks had left any footprints, they had already been wiped out by the fresh snowfall.

"We should never have left them!" wailed Blue. "Big Paulie is going to kill you."

"And you," Rory pointed out.

Blue wagged her flipper at him.

"No, just *you*. Paulie left *you* in charge, remember? He put all his trust in *you*."

Rory's stomach churned as if he'd eaten a bucket of rancid fish.

"Arghhhh! Paulie's going to kill me—he really is. He trusted me… What if the chicks were eaten by a killer whale?"

Blue grabbed him by the shoulders and shook him.

"Don't be silly! How would a killer whale get in here—unless it was dropped by parachute?"

"You never know; they're very intelligent," panicked Rory.

Blue made him sit down.

"Rory, shut your beak and do some deep-breathing exercises," she said, "Breathe in… and out. In… and out. Do you feel calmer now?"

"Erm, let me think about that… Nooooo!" he yelled, pulling his head feathers out. "The chicks couldn't have just disappeared into thin air—unless they've learned to fly?"

"Penguins can't fly," said Blue. "We don't have the right type of wings. Teeny and Tiny are probably just playing hide-and-seek behind those rocks."

They began to search frantically, which

immediately drew the attention of the bears.

"What are you looking for?" asked Orson.

"Nothing," said Rory casually. "Don't tell them, Blue."

"But we might be able to help," suggested Ursie.

It was most unusual for the bears to be helpful in any way. If anything, they were quite the opposite.

"We're fine, thank you," insisted Blue. "Go away, please."

They looked everywhere—behind every peak on the artificial cliff, behind each penguin hutch, and under the slide, but there was no sign of the chicks. Not so much as a piece of a fluffy feather.

"What if they're under the snow?" said Rory in alarm. "What if there was an avalanche off Paulie's roof and they're buried under it?"

Taking great care not to be seen by the boss, they skidded silently over to the palace to check. Unfortunately, the bears followed and called out to them at the top of their lungs.

"Try digging around with a stick!" yelled Orson, throwing an old walking cane into the penguin enclosure.

"Shhhh!" hissed Rory, terrified that Paulie would hear.

He took the stick and prodded miserably at the snowdrift.

"Give it a good poke!" shouted Ursie.

"That's what they do in those mystery programs on TV when they're looking for somebody."

"Please go away!" begged Blue.

Then Eddie and Clive turned up.

"What have you lost?" asked Clive, sliding down the hill on his bottom.

"*She* has lost her manners!" said Ursie, pointing his paw at Blue. "*She* keeps telling us to go away and we're only trying to help."

Rory took Clive to the side and told him what had happened.

"Paulie is going to kill you," said Clive matter-of-factly.

"If he does, can I have your snowboard, Rory?" asked Eddie.

Clive gave Rory a comforting slap on the back.

"It won't come to that; we'll help you look. Maybe Teeny and Tiny have gone to see the fairy penguins. Hatty and Brenda sometimes give them prawns."

"I love prawns," said Eddie, "Let's go and see."

The four of them hurried off and as they wandered into fairy-penguin territory, Eddie bumped into a giant snow-penguin in the shape of Muriel. To everyone's horror, its head fell off and rolled down the slope.

"Quick, run after it!" said Rory. "Stick it back on."

Eddie had almost done it when they heard whispering coming from Hatty's hutch.

"I bet the chicks are in there," muttered Rory. "I bet Muriel got Brenda and Hatty to grab them to get me into trouble."

He scraped the snow off the window with his flipper and pressed his face to the glass—and to Blue's surprise, he started giggling.

"What's so funny?" she whispered.

He moved aside so she could see. Blue's beak fell open.

Hatty and Brenda were holding up a life-sized cardboard penguin with a moustache. It was very badly drawn and rather a funny shape, but Muriel made it quite obvious who it was meant to be.

"Kiss me, Warren!" she swooned, wrapping

her flippers round its neck and gazing into its wonky eyes.

"Muriel just pecked him on the cheek!" squeaked Blue.

Eddie jostled her out of the way so that he could watch.

"Oooh... Is that Warren she's kissing? He's lost weight, hasn't he, Clive? It's probably because he's in love."

Clive rubbed the steam off the glass and peered inside.

"No, it's probably because he's made of cardboard, Eddie," he said.

This amused Eddie so much that he laughed out loud.

Hatty heard him first and quickly tapped Muriel on the shoulder.

"Ignore her, Warren," Muriel sighed. "She's just jealous of us."

It was only when Rory banged on the window that Muriel suddenly whipped round and realized that she was being watched.

"*What are you all looking at?*" she screeched as Brenda let them in. "I wasn't *kissing*, if that's what you thought. I was practicing my lifesaving skills, wasn't I, Hatty and Brenda?"

"You were? Oh, yes," spluttered Brenda. "In case Warren drowned."

"In kisses," giggled Hatty.

As Muriel was yelling angrily at her friends, Rory stopped laughing and began to search the hutch.

"Where have you hidden the emperor chicks, Muriel?" he demanded.

"And where have you hidden the prawns?" added Eddie.

By now, Blue had joined in the search. Furious at having her hutch invaded, Muriel stopped fighting with Brenda and Hatty and stood in Blue's way.

"How dare you look through my stuff, Bloop!" she shrieked. "Not that I've got anything to hide, have I, Hatty?"

"No," snorted Hatty. "Only your love letter to Warren."

Blue was losing patience.

"Seriously, Muriel, what have you done with the chicks? They must be here somewhere."

Seeing how anxious she looked, Muriel guessed what had happened… and her beak stretched into a nasty grin.

"Oh my cod! You've lost Teeny and Tiny, haven't you, Bloop?" she sneered. "Paulie is so going to kill you."

"No, he's going to kill me," said Rory.

"And when he does, I'm getting Rory's snowboard," announced Eddie cheerfully.

Rory put his head in his flippers.

"I'm in so much trouble."

"It's not over yet, Rory," said Blue. "If we all keep looking, we're bound to find them. You'll help us, won't you, Hatty and Brenda?"

They nodded enthusiastically.

"We love Teeny and Tiny," said Hatty.

"Teeny, Tiny!" said Brenda.

Muriel turned her back on them and preened her tail feathers. "Have fun, losers," she said scornfully.

Hatty and Brenda looked at her in dismay.

"Aren't you coming with us, Muriel?"

Muriel was about to say no when Blue interrupted her.

"Of course Muriel is coming... unless she wants Warren to find out about *Cardboard* Warren."

Muriel went pale.

"You wouldn't dare, Bloop!"

"Try me," said Blue, folding her flippers defiantly.

Seeing that she had no choice, Muriel pretended she'd been up for it all along and hurried everybody out of her hutch.

"Chop chop! What are you waiting for?" she snapped. "Just as well I'm coming. You guys couldn't organize a fish supper in a seafood shop, let alone a search par—"

She caught sight of the snow-Muriel.

"Oh my cod! My head's on back to front! *Who* did this to me?" she screeched.

"It wasn't Clive," said Eddie helpfully.

After some discussion, it was agreed that they should all go back to where Rory and Blue last saw the chicks and start the search from there, but this meant doing it under the prying eyes of the bears.

"Still looking for the emperor chicks?" bellowed Orson.

"No!" hissed Rory. "*Shush!*"

The last thing he wanted to do was alert Paulie, and Orson's voice could be heard on the other side of the zoo.

"We know something that you don't know," said Ursie. "Teeny and Tiny have been kidnapped."

"It's true," confirmed Orson. "While Rory and friends were frolicking on their snowboards, I distinctly heard somebody shouting, '*Help, kidnap!*'"

Rory stared at the bears as if he couldn't believe his ears.

"You're making it up—*kidnapped*? Why would anyone kidnap a penguin?"

Orson climbed down from his tree and explained.

"It happens all the time," he said. "Someone wants a waiter, they pick up a penguin. They want a butler, they take another penguin. Why? Because it's much cheaper than hiring a man in a black tuxedo."

"And they get them to pose for chocolate bars, and to dance on TV," added Ursie. "Though why they want to use silly penguins instead of handsome bears, I can't imagine. I've been able to dance like a pro since I was a cub, haven't I, Orson?"

45

Before Orson could reply, Ursie grabbed a hat and an umbrella that a visitor had dropped and went into a tap routine, singing along to keep the rhythm.

"A yatter ta da! A yatter ta da! A yatter... ta, yatter ta— Why isn't anyone watching?"

The penguins were far too busy getting their heads around the fact that the chicks had been kidnapped to admire Ursie's fancy footwork, and Rory told him so.

"Fine!" Ursie sulked. "Then you won't be interested to know what I can see over there!" he said, pointing with the umbrella.

"Correct," said Rory, going into a huddle with Clive and Eddie. "OK, guys, where shall we look next?"

"How about *over there!*" insisted Ursie, jabbing the umbrella in the same direction. "I can see them with my own eyes!"

"Watch it, you almost poked mine out," growled Orson. "Put that umbrella down... Ah yes, I can see the kidnappers—they look like two little girls."

"Thank you, Orson. That's because they *are* two little girls," snapped Ursie. "They're coming out of the gift shop carrying the chicks—but no one listens to me."

"You're joking," said Rory.

"Nope," said Ursie. "I'm a dancer, not a comedian."

Realizing that he was being completely serious, Rory went into a tailspin.

"Arghh…! Who…? How…?! Where are the kidnappers taking them?"

"How should I know?" snorted Ursie. "I'm not their father. They're making their way to the monkey house, but it could be a bathroom trip."

Rory chewed his flipper anxiously.

"Ursie, can you keep an eye on them, please, while I think what to do?" he pleaded. Ursie twirled his umbrella and pursed his hairy lips.

"Say pretty please."

Rory couldn't bring himself to do that, so Blue stepped forward.

"Pretty pretty pretty please… you old fur bag."

Ursie didn't hear the last bit, and

48

even Muriel laughed as he took the compliment.

"That's what I like to hear!" he said, shielding his eyes as he tried to follow the direction of the kidnappers. "The suspects have just taken a left turn into Pets' Corner…"

"What are we going to do, Rory?" wailed Blue.

"Less of the *we*," said Muriel. "What are *you* going to do, Rory? It's all your fault."

There was only one thing to do.

"I will stage a rescue!" he announced.

But the question was… *how*?

CHAPTER THREE

Penguin Pyramid

"You... stage a rescue?" scoffed Muriel. "Yeah, right. How are we even going to get out of the penguin enclosure, birdbrain? It's not like we're free-range."

"We'll dig a tunnel!" said Rory defensively. "I bet the chinstrap penguins have got a shovel in the stash of rubbish they've collected. I'll go and ask."

"Don't say anything to Warren about me," said Muriel hurriedly. "None of it is true, is it, Brenda?"

"Do you mean about the kissing?" said Brenda.

Muriel glared at her.

"I was *not* kissing!"

Rory made his way to Waldo's hutch and found him sitting with Wesley and Warren around a table. They were busy making something from odd pieces of lost property that visitors had left at the zoo over the years. They were a creative

group, but some of the things they made were so unusual, it was hard to tell what they were.

"Obviously it's a patchwork quilt, dear boy," explained Waldo. "Made entirely by flipper from potato chip bags, handkerchiefs,

and old sweaters. It's a gift for Mister and Missus Alaskadabra's new chick—it hatched yesterday, don't you know."

"I didn't," said Rory. "Did *you* know that Teeny and Tiny have been kidnapped?"

Waldo dropped a stitch.

"*No!* I'm shocked!"

"It just proves you can't leave anything lying around these days," said Wesley, snipping a square of wool out of a lost sweater.

"What are you going to do?" asked Warren, twirling the droopy fake moustache he insisted on wearing.

Rory cast his eyes around their hutch to see if there were any tools he could dig with, but apart from a box full of assorted cutlery and a pirate sword, there was nothing on display.

"I'm going to tunnel my way out and rescue them," said Rory, "Do you have a shovel I can borrow?"

The three chinstraps looked at each

other and muttered among themselves, as if the request was completely idiotic.

"A shovel is no use, lovey," explained Waldo. "The walls of your enclosure are made from reinforced concrete. It'd be easier to dig to Australia with a popsicle stick."

"What you need is *dynamite*," said Warren.

"Industrial explosives," suggested Wesley, rummaging through the contents of an old cookie tin. "Unfortunately, all we have in that department is this..."

He held up a small firework that had escaped from the park on bonfire night, unwrapped the blue paper, and peered down the end of the tube.

"Hmm… looks like it's used," he said apologetically. Have you got a Plan B?"

"Do you have a ladder?" asked Rory. "If we can't dig under, maybe we could climb over."

They couldn't find a ladder, but taking a fresh look at the objects scattered around the hutch, Rory noticed an old picnic table leaning against the wall.

"I could use that to make a ramp," he said. "If I lean it against the wall, I can snowboard up it and fly over the top."

Waldo wagged his flipper at him.

"Highly dangerous, dear. You can't go putting a ramp up willy-nilly or it'll collapse and then where will you be?"

"Up to your broken neck in snow," said Wesley. "Putting up ramps is a job for professionals."

"It's a good idea, though," said Warren. "You should work on it."

Rory's heart sank.

"But I don't know any professional rampers!"

Waldo rolled his eyes and put down the quilt.

"Yes, you do… us!" he tutted. "Warren, fetch the wrench. Wesley, get some nails. Rory, grab that baby stroller—I can use the handles to brace the ramp."

Helping the chinstraps carry all the things they needed, Rory struggled back to the rescue party through the snow.

Seeing Warren, Muriel got nervous and hid behind Hatty.

"Oh my cod! It's the real him!" she squeaked. "Hold me back, Brenda."

Eddie was far more interested in the table.

"Dude!" he said. "Are we having a picnic?"

"This is no picnic, believe me," said Waldo. "Hold the end of the tape measure while I figure out the distance between the wall and the ramp."

Clive scratched his head.

"Why are you making a ramp?"

"Plan B," said Rory. "We're going to snowboard over the top to find the chicks."

While Blue and the rockhoppers were thrilled by the idea, Muriel wasn't so keen. She was a good swimmer, but snow stunts weren't really her thing.

"That's a stupid idea. Isn't it a stupid idea, Brenda and Hatty?"

Rory shrugged.

"Warren thought it was good."

Muriel's eyes flicked across to Warren. He was doing something with his wrench and she melted.

"Like I was saying, it's a brilliant idea. Now get out of Warren's way and let him build the thing."

The penguins watched as Warren and Wesley built the ramp under Waldo's expert guidance. While Rory passed the

hammer and held the
nails, the bears kept up
a running commentary
on the kidnappers'
whereabouts.

"They have left
Pets' Corner!"
announced Orson.

"They have just stopped for a crêpe," added Ursie.

"I wish I had time to stop for a crêpe," muttered Waldo. "No matter. Pass the wrench, Warren. I need to check my nuts and bolts—I don't want them coming undone."

Having finished the safety check, Waldo stood back and admired his handiwork.

"It's leaning too far to the right," said Wesley.

"I'll adjust the braces," said Warren.

Muriel sighed. "Catch me, Hats, I'm swooning."

A long time and a lot of huffing and puffing later, Waldo declared that the ramp was finished. It looked a bit rickety to Rory, but he felt responsible for losing the chicks, so he offered to test it.

"Good luck," said Blue. "You can do it."

He hoped she couldn't see his knees trembling. The ramp was leaning too far to the left now, but he had to hurry as the braces were slowly sinking into the snow.

"The kidnappers have finished their crêpe. They're heading toward the Animal Adventure Center," warned Orson.

"They're gathering speed... Get a move on, Rory!" bellowed Ursie.

Rory dragged his snowboard to the top of the slide. Taking a deep breath, he pushed off with his flippers and hurtled

along the black ice. But as he flew off the end and hit the makeshift ramp at thirty miles per hour, there was a loud crash and the whole thing collapsed, burying him under a heap of wood, metal, and springs.

"It must have had a screw loose," remarked Warren.

"It's not the only one," said Muriel, glaring at Rory. "Honestly, Bloop, Warren makes us a lovely ramp and your boyfriend goes and breaks it."

"Ouch… splinters," groaned Rory, rubbing his tail. "Now what are we going to do?"

"I could get them out with my sewing needle," suggested Waldo eagerly.

"Forget my splinters," said Rory, "how are we going to get out of here?"

There was talk of making a new ramp out of ice by packing the snow down and polishing it with their feet, but according to Waldo, it was the wrong sort of snow.

Meanwhile, the kidnappers were getting away and if it hadn't been for

Blue's sudden idea, the emperor chicks might have been lost forever.

"I've got it!" she whooped.

"Ugh, don't give it to me," winced Muriel.

Blue ignored her and explained her idea to Hatty and Brenda.

"Do you remember when we did our synchronized swimming act for the talent show and made a penguin pyramid in the pool?"

It wasn't something they could forget in a hurry.

"I remember," grimaced Hatty. "Muriel made us throw you up in the air really high, didn't she?"

"Yes," frowned Brenda, "really, really high, even when we weren't in the water."

"Exactly!" continued Blue. "And there were only three of us then. Imagine how high we could get if all of us formed a pyramid—we could reach the top of the wall and jump over!"

She studied the heights and weights of the group of assorted penguins and came up with a plan.

"OK, the chinstraps should be at the bottom with Eddie and Clive standing on their shoulders; Hatty and Brenda, you need to stand on the rockhopper boys and I'll stand on Muriel."

"You are *not* standing on me, Bloop," insisted Muriel.

"I think it's a marvellous idea," said Warren.

"You *are* standing on me, Bloop," said Muriel, batting her eyelashes at him, "then if Rory climbs up the pyramid, he can sit on the wall and pull us all up. Admit it, I'm a genius."

Blue seethed in silence. Muriel had completely stolen her idea and taken the credit for it, but there was no time to be particular. If they didn't get over the wall soon, the chicks would have left the zoo and might never be found again.

"Come along, Wesley and Warren!" said Waldo, clapping his hands. "Let's make a nice, firm bottom. Everybody form a pyramid."

Being the least athletic, the chinstraps braced themselves to make a steady

base while the rockhoppers and the fairy penguins piled on top of each other using their legendary acrobatic skills. Blue, being the lightest, was passed up to Brenda and Hatty, who flung her into the air. She somersaulted and landed neatly on Muriel's shoulders.

"Hurry! The kidnappers are turning left past the parrot house…" urged Orson.

Rory took a deep breath and started to climb the penguin pyramid.

"*Oooof!* Mind where you're putting your foot, dear boy," squeaked Waldo. "You kicked me in the tail feather."

"The whole thing's wobbling!" bellowed Ursie. "The pyramid is collapsing; Rory is going to die!"

CHAPTER FOUR

Penguins on the Loose

"**I**'m too young to die!" yelled Rory. "Grab my ankles, Blue!"

It was hard to grab anything with flippers, let alone a penguin struggling to climb on to such little shoulders, but somehow Blue managed to trap Rory's feet by pressing them against her ears. After a nail-biting wobble, he regained his balance and pulled himself up onto the wall. As Blue, Muriel, Hatty, and Brenda clung to each other's waists and scrabbled with their toes, Rory hauled them up, followed by Clive and Eddie.

The fairy penguins and the rockhoppers, however, were a lot lighter than the chinstraps.

"We'll stay here, darlings," said Waldo, falling back into the enclosure. "We'll only slow you down."

"Be careful how you go, you sweet, brave penguins," added Wesley.

"I do so admire you," said Warren.

"Ditto!" murmured Muriel dreamily.

The brown bears came over to give them some encouragement, but it backfired.

"Take care; it's a big, scary world out there," said Orson.

"Unless you're a bear," added Ursie. "Nothing eats bears."

"But lots of things eat penguins," said Orson. "Good luck! The kidnappers are heading that way," he pointed out. "Aim for the Animal Adventure Center."

The penguins were already nervous. They had never been out of the enclosure before and had no idea what to expect. They knew certain animals lived there because they'd heard them roar, bark, and shriek, but they had never actually seen them. The camel in particular came as a shock to Muriel.

"Oh my cod!" she screamed. "There's a huge woolly thing with bumps."

"They're humps," said Brenda, studying the information panel nailed to the fence. "Bactrian camels have two and dromedaries have one—it says so here."

Muriel stared at her in amazement. The idea that Brenda could read was an even greater shock than the camel.

"Brenda, how dare you read stuff!" she scolded. "Hatty, you better not be able to read."

"Me? No, Brenda is much smarter than I am," fibbed Hatty.

For once, Muriel was speechless, which was just as well. The last thing the rescuers needed was to draw attention to themselves. There were visitors walking around and if they saw the penguins on the loose, they'd be bound to tell the zookeeper and he'd come and capture them.

"Quick, hide behind the hedge!" hissed Rory as a teacher walked past with a line of schoolchildren. "Brenda, we need you to read the signposts and direct us to the Animal Adventure Center."

"Brains before beauty," grumbled Muriel, giving Brenda a shove.

Luckily, the Animal Adventure Center wasn't far away. It was just past the ring-tailed lemur enclosure and it was lunchtime, so most of the visitors were in the restaurant. With some ducking and diving, the penguins sneaked in undetected.

"Look, Clive," hissed Eddie, peering into an enclosure littered with lettuce and chopped fruit. "Someone has dropped a *massive* pie in there. I wonder if it's a fish pie?"

Eddie licked his beak, then leaped back as the pie grew four scaley legs and a head.

"Ohhh... it's a pie with a *face!*" he shrieked, hiding behind Clive.

"It's a giant tortoise," read Brenda. "It says here it came from the Galapagos Islands and it's a hundred years old— that's probably why it walks so slowly."

"Well, we need to get a move on," urged Rory, "if we're going to rescue the chicks. We can't stop at every animal we see or— Muriel, what are you doing?"

She was poking her beak through the wire mesh of a long enclosure decorated with logs and bark, which startled the small furry creature that lived there, so that it lifted its stripy tail and squirted her.

Muriel clutched her nostrils and gagged. "*Eughh...* that stunk!"

"It's a *skunk*, not a stunk," stated Brenda.

"You've read it wrong," choked Muriel. "It must be a stunk—it stinks!"

The other penguins hurried over to see what the fuss was about and found the skunk looking deeply offended.

"I don't smell, do I?" it said, sniffing its armpits. "I groomed myself from top to bottom this morning."

"Believe me, you forgot your bottom," said Muriel. "And you really need to change your perfume... *Phwoarrrr...* you've done it *again!*"

"That was me," boasted Eddie.

Rory was getting very annoyed with his rescue party. They seemed to have forgotten their mission and were behaving as if they were on a day trip. He couldn't help thinking it was selfish of them, given that *he* was the one Paulie was going to kill if they didn't find the chicks. He was about to hurry them along when he was distracted by the antics of some rodent-like creatures living in a sandy pit furnished with rocks and artificial termite mounds.

"Meerkats," Brenda informed them.

"You're kidding," said Rory.

He had never seen one before, but he'd always been jealous of meerkats.

It was well known that they were one of the most popular breeds in the zoo—something the bears never grew tired of telling him. Apparently, people found them cute and cuddly, but Rory couldn't imagine why.

"I don't get it, Blue," he said as the meerkats stood on sentry duty on the lookout for stray eagles. "How are they cuter than penguins?"

Blue watched them for a moment.

"I don't get it either, Rory. I bet they can't even snowboard."

Muriel waddled over to the pit and confronted the meerkats head-on.

"Seriously?" she scoffed. "*You* are our competition for cute?"

In reply, the meerkats
lay on their backs to show off
their fluffy tummies, and juggled
pebbles with their feet.

"So fluffy!" sighed Brenda.

"So juggly," agreed Hatty.

"So what?" snapped Muriel. "We can
out-cute them any day."

Her head was suddenly turned by
a wandering peacock who chose that
moment to shake his dramatic tail
feathers at her.

"Show-off!" said Muriel. "I'm not
interested."

The peacock looked down at her.

"Nor am I! I've seen a better tail on a
guinea pig. I was simply going to suggest

that you hold a 'Cute-Off'—meerkats versus penguins. The skunk, the tortoise, and I will judge who's the cutest."

Rory threw his flippers up in exasperation.

"We don't have time to play games!"

He stamped his foot to make his point, slipped on the ice and landed hard on his rump with his feet in the air.

"Now...that's...what...I...call...cute!" smiled the tortoise.

The peacock and the skunk agreed— and it was one to nothing in favor of the penguins.

There was no stopping them now, but the meerkats were equally determined to win the competition. Making the sweetest faces, they lined up in a row like can-can dancers and assumed their lookout poses.

"The meerkats get my vote!" called the skunk.

"Shush, Stinky!" said Muriel. "We're so sweet, you'll need fillings. Hatty, Brenda, and Bloop—hold flippers!"

"Ah," said Hatty, "friends!"

"Cute friends," said Brenda.

Blue clamped her flippers firmly to her sides.

"Hold flippers? Oh, come on, this is sappy!"

"Just waddle, Bloop!" muttered Muriel. "Stick your bottom out. There is no way I'm losing to those cheesy scraps of fur."

Grabbing hold of Blue, Hatty, and Brenda, she jerked the fairy penguins across the snow, making them stumble and totter.

"Aw...they look so cute when they waddle, don't they, Clive?" said Eddie.

"Get a grip," said Clive.

But happily for the girls, the peacock, the tortoise, and the skunk agreed with Eddie and awarded them ten out of ten.

After Clive and Eddie had done a break-dance, it looked as if the penguins had the cute-off in the bag. But then the opposition pulled out their trump card—a baby meerkat!

Its mother held it up by the armpits and swung it gently backward and forward.

It cooed, chuckled, sucked its toes, and for a grand finale, waved shyly to the judges and blew them a kiss.

"You...cutie...pie...Melt...my...
heart...why...don't...you?" sighed the
tortoise.

"I just want to squeeze him and hug him!" said the skunk.

"I just want to slap him," said Muriel.

"He's not cute. I'll tell you what's cute—have you ever seen an emperor chick?"

The peacock drew himself up to his full height.

"I have, as matter of fact. I saw two emperor chicks a few moments ago and I remember thinking how odd it was that they were out of their enclos—"

Rory's heart skipped a beat.

"You saw them? Were they with two little girls?"

The peacock fanned himself with his magnificent tail, then nodded.

"They were heading toward the aquarium."

"You've probably just saved my life," breathed Rory, gathering the rescue party around him. "The chicks went that way; follow me!"

"Actually, it was *that* way," said the mother meerkat, pointing in the opposite direction. "Oh, you are one *cute* penguin!"

CHAPTER FIVE

Snakes and Sardines

"Quick, I can see the kidnappers!" shouted Rory, rallying his troops. "Keep your heads down and make a run for it."

As the penguins approached, the two little girls tried to go through the aquarium doors at the same time and were delayed for a few moments when their doll's strollers locked together. As they shifted them in an attempt to disentangle the wheels, Rory saw the chicks bouncing under the blankets. "At least they're alive and well," he said. "The kidnappers have tucked them up under the covers. I hope they don't get too warm."

Muriel made clucking noises at him.

"What are you, a mother hen?" she teased. "You are so in touch with your feminine side—isn't he, Brenda?"

Brenda didn't agree, but as she was already in trouble for being intelligent, she didn't want to make Muriel angrier with her.

"Yes, Rory is so in touch with his mother," said Hatty.

"He's a... feminine hen," suggested Brenda.

Blue dismissed their comments with a wave of her flipper.

"It's nice that Rory cares," she said. "You should try it sometime, Muriel."

By this time, the kidnappers had disappeared into the aquarium.

Looking around to make sure no visitors were lurking, the penguins darted inside. It was a lot darker in there than they'd expected, but the tanks were illuminated. Having never seen fish swimming in tanks before, Clive wasn't sure they were real and tapped on the glass.

"Maybe it's a TV," he commented, "like the ones Orson and Ursie told us about."

As cubs, the bears had been bottle-fed by the zookeeper's wife at home in front of the television. They had fond memories of watching it and could often be heard singing the theme tune from one of the shows.

"It was called *BeastEnders*," Orson told them. "It was like a wildlife program, only with people eating, fighting, and having babies."

Eddie's stomach rumbled as he watched a group of juicy sardines swimming around their rocks.

"If this is TV, it's my favorite," he said. "It's the food channel."

"That's not TV, silly," said Muriel hungrily. "Those fish are real and it's way past dinnertime. Brenda and Hatty, give me a leg up. I'm going in!"

Rory watched in horror as Brenda and Hatty formed a pyramid with Eddie, and tossed Muriel into the air. She hit her head on the ceiling and, slightly dazed, belly-flopped into the massive tank with a *splash*, causing the sardines to scatter.

After a few seconds, Muriel found her bearings and, diving like a pro, she began to chase the fish.

"Oooh... I really don't think Muriel should be in there," said Brenda, reading the information plaque. "The fish aren't the only thing in that tank. See that word there, Hatty? The one that begins with an 'L'?"

Hatty screwed up her eyes, read it, and gasped.

"L... E... *Eek!* Those things are huge! I'm sure they eat penguins, Brenda."

"I'm sure they do too, Hatty," agreed Brenda.

They banged on the side of the tank to alert Muriel, but she was too busy showing off to notice. It was then that the sardines decided they'd had quite enough of being chased, and tried to scare Muriel off.

"It is a foolish penguin who dives into a tank in which a leopard seal lives!" they burbled.

"Leopard seal? Yeah, right, I'm not falling for that old trick," grinned Muriel.

"It's behind you!" chorused the sardines.

Muriel was about to laugh in their fishy faces when she caught sight of Hatty and Brenda gesturing wildly at her to get out. As she turned, she saw a huge shadowy form looming toward her through the greenish gloom. It was getting nearer and nearer.

"Oh my cod, oh my cod!" she panicked. "It's a leop—It's a seal... It's going to eat me! *Heeeeelp!*"

The sardines scattered as Muriel flailed around in fright.

"Swim, Muriel! Swim to the top!" shouted Rory.

Pinching her nostrils, she shot to the surface and bobbed about like a cork with the giant creature nibbling at her heels. Screaming and spluttering, she scrabbled out of the tank, slid down the side in a soggy heap, and fainted.

When she awoke, she thought she'd died and gone to penguin hell as Brenda and Hatty stood over her, fanning her face with their flippers.

"Leopard seal," she cheeped feebly. "Leopard seal."

"It's a leatherback turtle," said Blue.

"They're harmless to penguins. Look, he's waving at you."

Muriel sat up, glared at the friendly turtle and made a very rude gesture, only to notice that all the sardines were staring at her, open-mouthed. She caught sight of her reflection in the glass and screeched.

"Don't look at me! I'm having a bad-feather day! Brenda, book me in for a blow-dry *now!"*

Hiding her soggy, seaweed-covered head under both flippers, she skidded off, pausing only to scream as she bashed into the shark tank, causing the shark to bare rows of dagger-like teeth. The other penguins hurried after her.

"Come back, Muriel!" panted Rory. "The kidnappers went the other way— we're going to lose them!"

But Muriel shot out of the aquarium and didn't stop until she was exhausted, by which time the penguins found themselves in a completely different animal house. Again, it was full of large tanks, but there was very little water in any of them. In fact, they were decorated with branches, vines and bark.

"Where are we, Rory?" asked Blue.

Not wishing to admit he was lost, Rory studied the tank nearby to see if he could see any animals, but the tank looked empty.

"Reptile house," read Brenda.

The penguins stared at each other blankly. They had learned the names of lots of different species from Orson and Ursie, but neither bear had ever mentioned reptiles.

"I bet reptiles are small and furry," guessed Eddie.

There was a dead mouse in the tank in front of them, but penguins knew mice when they saw them. Mice often had their babies under the floorboards of Paulie's palace.

"Mice must be reptiles," said Eddie, "right, Clive?"

As if to prove him wrong, something shifted in the tank.

Brenda studied the nameplate.

"Anacond—*Arghhh!*" she wailed as a snake, as thick as an elephant's leg and as long as the penguin slide, began to uncoil. It flicked its forked tongue and shot forward. As the penguins shot back, the creature unhinged its jaws, displayed its wicked curved fangs and swallowed the mouse whole. First the head disappeared, then the body, then the tail.

The penguins watched in horror as the anaconda's lunch traveled in a mouse-shaped lump toward its stomach, which was so large, it could easily hold several penguins. With this in mind, they waddled off in silence, punctuated by the odd squeak and scream as they came across more scary, scaley things with far too many teeth.

"Alligat— *Arghhh!*"

"Komod— *Ohhhh...* dragons!"

"Spitting cobra... *Arghhh!*"

They blundered out through the fire exit and then, to their great relief, the penguins found themselves back outside in the snowy sunlight—but where were they? Even more importantly, where were the kidnappers?

Muriel gave Brenda a poke.

"Come along, Miss Clever. Read the signs!"

But there weren't any signs and no sign of Teeny and Tiny either.

Blue had a word with Rory.

"What shall we do? I'm getting really worried about the chicks—aren't you?"

Rory nodded, and with a deep sigh, he wondered how Paulie was going to kill him.

CHAPTER SIX

Hippo-hoppomus

"**A**dmit it, Rory," said Muriel, "we'll never find the chicks now."

But he refused to listen.

"We have to keep looking. I'm not giving up."

"Clive is giving up," said Eddie. "He just told me he was hungry and fed up and wanted to go home because it was all a big waste of time, didn't you, Clive?"

Clive shuffled awkwardly.

"It does seem kind of pointless, Rory," he admitted. "The zoo is huge and the kidnappers could be anywhere. By the time we get to the other side, they'll be gone."

"Let's put it to a vote," said Muriel. "All those in favor of missing dinner for no good reason, put your flippers up."

Without hesitation, Blue held up both flippers, but she was the only one. If Muriel hadn't pinned Hatty and Brenda's flippers to their sides, Rory might have had more support, but he was facing a vote of no confidence.

"I'll carry on without you then," he said.

"Let's hope Paulie finishes you off quickly," said Muriel, hanging back with Brenda and Hatty.

"Paulie won't really kill you, Rory," reassured Blue. "He's all beak."

"He'll just be so angry, you'll die of fright," cackled Muriel.

Blue was just about to remind Muriel about Cardboard Warren when a peculiar, patterned head appeared from out of the clouds.

"*Reptiiiiile!*" screamed Muriel, jumping into Clive's flippers.

"G-i-r-a-f-f-e spells 'giraffe'," said Brenda.

The giraffe gazed at the penguins from under the thick fringes of her eyelashes and blew on them gently.

"What are you dear little waddly things doing so far from home? I can see your enclosure from here and you don't appear to be in it… Why is that?"

She bent her long neck, put her fuzzy, tulip-shaped ear next to Rory's beak, and listened carefully as he explained about the kidnappers.

"Two little girlies, you say?" she mooed softly. "With doll strollers? Let me see."

Stretching her neck to its full extent, she swiveled her head like a periscope and scanned the zoo for anybody matching that description.

"Aha! Do they have blonde hair and pink strollers?" she asked. "Because if so, they're over there, heading toward the lions."

Rory was all for racing off at once, but as Blue pointed out, the lion enclosure was on the far side of the zoo.

"We've only got short legs," she said. "It'll be dark by the time we get there."

The giraffe lowered her great head over the fence and rested her chin on the snow.

"Hop on," she said. "I'll give you a lift to the ape house—they'll take you from there."

The penguins exchanged glances. It was a long way up and, not surprisingly, they had never ridden a giraffe before.

"Rory, what if she charges like a rhinoceros?" asked Blue anxiously.

The giraffe heard and smiled sweetly.

"There's no charge," she said. "I'll do it for free. Who wants to sit in the front?"

"Me," said Muriel, pushing Hutty and Brenda aside. "I'll get travel sick on the back."

The penguins climbed onto the giraffe. As they clung to her horns and stiff mane, she ambled gracefully across her paddock, taking great care not to stumble and upset them. From up there, the penguins could see all four corners of the zoo.

"Wow, what a fantastic view!" said
Rory. "Look at that, Blue."

"Eyes shut tight," squeaked Blue, not daring to look.

When the giraffe got to the other side, she stopped and lowered her head over a moat into a field full of trees, climbing frames, and ropes.

"Would all passengers traveling to the lions please change here," she said. "Remember to take all your belongings with you and have a safe journey."

As the penguins slid down her neck, a family of chimpanzees came bounding over.

"Oh my cod, somebody's armpits need a trim," remarked Muriel.

The father chimp spoke to the giraffe; then walking on long legs with his arms

111

above his head, he suddenly dropped to the floor and rolled head over heels toward the cluster of penguins.

"Ugh, hairy pits *and* a bald bottom," gulped Muriel. "Bad combo."

Before she could criticize him further, the chimp scooped her up in his huge leathery hand, clamped her in the crook of his armpit, then swung into the nearest tree.

"Help! *Phwoarrr*, someone forgot his deodorant. Hatty, Brenda, don't just stand there!" she screamed as the great ape paused to pick his nose.

As she spoke, Hatty and Brenda were scooped up by the mother chimp and, one by one, all the penguins were passed in a relay from chimp to chimp, swinging from tree to tree.

"Whoo hoo!" whooped Rory. "I'm flying!"

He was almost sorry when they got to the other side, which is more than could be said for Muriel, who had turned a funny shade of green.

"I lost my breakfast," she retched. "I have it all over my feathers—Hatty, get it off, get it off!" she stamped. "Brenda, hold me, I think I'm going to barf again. *Bloooargh!*"

The chimpanzee waited patiently for Muriel to calm down, then ushered her gently toward the moat that went under a bridge and formed a pool in the next paddock. The ice in the moat had been smashed into tiny icebergs so that the chimps couldn't cross it, but a penguin could easily swim through.

"Dive in, Muriel," urged Rory.

Muriel stuck one toe into the water and pulled it out again.

"Brrr… No, *you* dive in. What if it leads to the leopard-seal pool?"

Rory waddled over to the edge.

"If the seal doesn't get me, Paulie will!"

He jumped in and disappeared under the bridge and Blue leaped straight in after him.

"I'm coming with you, Rory!"

They popped up in a lake full of frosty lily pads and large gray stepping stones. To their relief, there was no sign of a leopard seal.

"Hey, Eddie! Clive! Come on in, the water's lovely!" called Rory, "It's OK, Muriel. It's perfectly safe. There are no animals here."

Blue noticed massive fresh hoofprints in the snow at the edge of the bank and frowned.

"Are you sure about that, Rory?"

But it was too late. Just as Muriel bobbed up in the murky pool with Hatty and Brenda, one of the stepping stones moved.

Muriel froze and gingerly tapped Brenda on the shoulder.

"Please tell me I'm seeing things, Brenda."

"Hip-hip…" stammered Brenda, trying to read the notice.

"Hooray?" said Eddie.

"Ignore her, she's just got hiccups," said Muriel. "Stop showing off, Brenda."

But Brenda was just trying to read a difficult word from a long distance.

"Hip... po... potamus!" she blurted.

Hearing its name, the nearest hippo rose to the surface, blowing bubbles through its nose, and looked at the penguins.

"Oh," it remarked flatly. "I'd hoped you were cabbages. We usually get cabbage on Friday."

Seeing that the hippos were vegetarians and wished them no harm, Rory swam over to Blue.

"I have an idea," he whispered. "We could hop across their big backs to the other side; pass it on!"

So Blue whispered it to Hatty, Hatty whispered it to Brenda, and Brenda whispered it to Muriel, but by the time the message got to Eddie, it made very little sense.

"We should shop for lots of snacks while the others hide?" repeated Eddie excitedly. "Count me in, I'm starving!"

"Just follow me," groaned Rory. Hopping from hippo to hippo, they made it to the other side without a hitch, and having squeezed under the barrier, they came out opposite the lions.

"Look! There are the kidnappers!" squealed Blue.

Parked in front of the enclosure were two doll strollers, and standing on a bench, were two little girls holding emperor chicks.

The bad news was, they were dangling them right over the lion pit.

CHAPTER SEVEN

The Penguins
are Stuffed

The penguins hid behind a garbage bin and watched with mounting horror as the little girls held the chicks over the railings by their feet.

"I can't see any lions, can you, Chicky?" said the girl on the right, holding the chick in her outstretched arms. "Maisie, can your chick see the lion?"

"Dunno," said her friend. "I'll swing him so he can get a better look."

It was more than Muriel could bear.

"Their mothering skills are even worse than yours, Bloop. Don't just stand there!"

Forgetting to hide, she raced toward the girls, screeching and gnashing her beak.

"No, Muriel!" wailed Rory.

Startled by a crazy bird jumping on to their bench, the girls screamed and dropped the chicks, who tumbled through the air and landed at the bottom of the lion pit.

As the girls ran off in tears, Rory raced over to the railings, hardly daring to look. It was such a long drop; could two little chicks survive a fall like that?

"Oh no... oh dear... They must have broken their necks!" he gasped. "If the fall didn't kill them, the lions will! Where are they?"

He shouted their names.

"Teeny? Tiny? Can you hear me?"

There was no reply. Muriel went into shock and became hysterical, waddling in circles.

"The chicks are in with the lions; lions are worse than leopard seals and snakes and sharks and—"

Blue slapped her on the beak.

"Calm down, Muriel. We have to stay calm. Maybe the lions are asleep. Maybe the chicks landed in soft snow."

She ran and poked her beak through the bars further along.

"I can see them—there they are!"

Teeny and Tiny were lying face down in a dish next to the lions' den.

"They're probably just stunned," Blue murmured, but she wasn't certain.

"Rory, this is all your fault!" yelled Muriel. "Isn't it Rory's fault and not mine that the chicks fell in, Brenda and Hatty?"

"Poor Teeny; she was so tiny," wept Brenda.

"Poor Tiny; he was so teeny," snivelled Hatty.

Rory stood on the bench and began to climb over the railings.

"I'm going in there," he announced. "I'm going to rescue the chicks or die trying."

Blue grabbed him and pulled him back down.

"Don't do it, Rory! The fall will kill you! The chicks are so light, they drifted down, but you will drop like a stone."

"Oh, *balloons!*" he said.

"No need to swear," said Eddie.

"When I said balloons, I *meant* balloons," said Rory. "Look!"

There was a kiosk nearby that sold helium balloons with A GIFT FROM CITY ZOO printed on the front. There were hundreds of them, bobbing on strings.

"If I held on to some balloons, I could float down, grab the chicks, and slip back out through the railings at the bottom," said Rory.

"Brilliant!" said Blue. "I'll grab a bunch, but I need someone to weigh me down or I'll float up into the sky."

"Off you go, Hatty," said Muriel, grabbing Hatty's blubber. "You're nice and heavy."

"At least she's nice," said Blue. "Come on, guys, it'll take more than one penguin to hold me down."

Making sure that no one saw them, the volunteers edged their way over to the kiosk and Clive acted as lookout while Blue pecked through the balloon strings.

Despite all his worries, Rory couldn't help smiling as she bounced back with the balloons, the others clinging on to her ankles to prevent her from taking off.

"Thanks, Blue," he said. "But why two bunches? One will do."

"I'm coming with you," she said bravely, tying the balloon strings round her waist.

"No way," he said. "This is my mess."

"Our mess," corrected Blue.

As they teetered together on the edge of the railing with the wind tugging at the balloons, Rory reached out and held her flipper.

"If we die, I just want you to know you're the best ever, Blue."

"Oh, puh-lease," said Muriel, "I think
I'm going to be sick again."

Rory and Blue jumped.

"I can't look!" said Clive.

"It's all right, I'll look for you," said
Eddie. "They're floating down... down...
down... Whoops, here comes a lion!"

Clive's eyes sprang open.

"Lion! Where? Noooooo... Rory's my best friend!"

"Just joking, Clive," said Eddie. "Hang on... I thought *I* was your best friend..."

Landing safely, Blue and Rory let go of the balloons, then scrambled off and hid inside a thicket of grass. The chicks were lying right by the lions' den about fifty feet away.

"They're not moving, Rory," said Blue.

"It's hard to tell from here," he replied, trying to stay positive. "Maybe they're asleep. Maybe they're just keeping still so the lions don't notice them."

"What if the lions notice *us*, Rory?"

He looked all around. There was still no sign of the beasts. He had often heard them roaring, and if they were anything like as fierce as they sounded, he really didn't want to bump into them.

"They're probably all asleep in their den after a heavy lunch," said Rory. "Stay there while I make a dash for the chicks before the lions wake up."

Blue shook her head.

"You can't carry both of them. Let's go on the count of three—and stay under cover! One... two... three!"

Blue and Rory inched out from the grass, zigzagging on their bellies across the snow. Shifting from hiding place to hiding place, they edged their way over to the chicks.

"Teeny?" hissed Blue. "Tiny?"

The chicks lay still and silent.

"I'll try beak-to-beak resuscitation," said Rory. "There was a medical program on Waldo's radio. It said to pinch their nostrils and blow into their beaks."

"I'll turn them over," said Blue.

Very gently, she brushed the snow from Tiny's back, but as soon as she felt his little body she drew her flipper back. Rory's heart started to pound.

"What's wrong, Blue?"

She couldn't speak. She reached out with a shaking flipper, prodded Teeny and groaned. The feathers stood up on the back of Rory's neck.

"Please don't tell me they're dead. I'll never forgive myself."

He gazed at Blue urgently. She didn't look sad; she looked angry. She picked the chicks up roughly and stood them on their feet.

"They were never alive, Rory... They're stuffed *toys!*"

He slumped down and stared into their glass eyes. He touched their felt beaks and their fur fabric. There was no getting away from it.

"We've been fooled!" he groaned. "The bears swore they saw the kidnappers coming out of the gift shop with emperor chicks."

"Duh," said Blue. "They sell toy animals in there."

Rory kicked himself.

"How could I be so stupid, Blue?"

Blue lifted one of the toy chicks and examined the neat stitching.

"They're very realistic, Rory," she said. "I fell for it too. We *all* did."

But something else was troubling him. If the real chicks weren't in the lion pit, where were they? He was just wondering if there was any chance of finding them again when he heard a commotion coming from above.

"Look out!" yelled Clive.

"It's behind yoooou!" pointed Eddie.

There was a low growl. Rory and Blue turned slowly. Standing right behind them was an enormous lion—and it was licking its lips.

CHAPTER EIGHT

Go, Muriel

"**K**eep… very… still," whispered Rory, clamping his knees together to stop from trembling. "If we keep very still, maybe the lion won't notice us."

Blue glared at him.

"What, because black and white is such a great camouflage against the snow?"

"Maybe it will think we're zebras," said Rory hopefully.

Blue put her flippers over her eyes.

"Lions *eat* zebras!"

The lion pawed the ground and prowled a little closer. Up above, what was left of the rescue party had a bird's-eye view of the situation and it didn't look good.

"Look out, Rory, it's creeping closer!" called Clive, clapping his flippers to scare the lion.

"Shoo, cat! Scat!"

"Yeah!" said Eddie. "Poo, fat cat!"

Muriel gave them a withering look.

"Shoo, cat? Poo, fat cat? You two couldn't scare a day-old kitten."

Clive turned on her.

"Muriel, if you hadn't scared the kidnappers, they'd never have dropped the chicks, and Rory and Blue wouldn't be in the lion pit."

"That is *sooo* unfair!" she said. "If Rory and Bloop are dumb enough to jump into a cage with LIONS written on it, how is that my fault? L-O-I-N-S spells 'lions.' I'm right, aren't I, Brenda?"

"That spells 'loins,' actually," said Brenda, refusing to look at her.

"Loins… lions… They're the same thing, aren't they, Hatty? *Hatty*, talk to me!"

Hatty put her head under her flipper and refused to reply. And then Muriel realized that even Eddie had got it in for her.

"Clive," said Eddie. "If Warren finds out that Muriel got everyone killed, he'll never want to kiss her, will he?"

"Someone's bound to tell him," said Clive.

Aghast, Muriel stopped preening and stomped off toward the kiosk. Brenda and Hatty trudged after her, but she waved them away.

"Leave me alone. I know who my friends are," she said.

Down below, the lion was circling Rory and Blue. Occasionally, it stopped to spray its scent on a tree, but it was coming closer and closer.

"Let's try and outrun it," whispered Rory. "It's not like it's a cheetah. Orson told me that cheetahs are the fastest cats on four legs."

"And *I'm* telling you we're the slowest birds on two!" quivered Blue. "Look how long its legs are! Look at the size of its paws!"

"I'd rather not," said Rory. "I know! What if we tell it we're friends of Paulie? It won't dare to eat us then, will it?"

Anything was worth a try.

"Excuse me, Mister Lion…" he began.

Blue held his beak shut.

"Don't call him that, you'll anger him! Lions like to think they are kings of the jungle. You have to call him 'Your Majesty'."

The lion shook its mane and gave a spine-tingling roar.

"I'm not talking to him if he's going to be like that," muttered Rory. "What's he doing now?"

The lion was down on its haunches, thrashing its tail.

"It's going to pounce," bleated Blue. "This is the end. Hold me, Rory."

He clung to Blue as hard as he could.

"I'll never let go of you," he said "It will have to eat us together."

As they said their last goodbyes, the lion sprang…

…but in mid-flight, it suddenly let out a

yelp and veered off,
clutching its snout.

It had been hit by
a lump of ice the size
of a baseball that had
fallen mysteriously
from the sky.

"Kitty! *Take that!*"
said a familiar voice.

It was Muriel.
She was floating
down into the lion
pit on a bunch of
balloons armed with
snowballs.

"M-O-O-R-I-E-L... Go, Muriel! Go, Muriel!" chanted Hatty and Brenda.

As Muriel landed on top of the lions' den, the others heard her shouting back, "That's not how you spell it! It's Muriel with a 'U'!"

"Go, Uriel, Go Uriel!" they sang encouragingly.

The lion looked up from nursing its nose. Spotting a penguin on the roof, it gave a thunderous roar, ran toward the den, and began to climb up the ladder.

"Get down, you overgrown cat!" screeched Muriel, pelting it with snowballs. "Run, Bloop! Rory, go the other way... Confuse it!"

Blue skidded toward the bars at the bottom of the lion pit, hoping to slip through them to safety, but the snow had drifted into a thick heap, blocking her way.

"Help me dig, Rory!" she panted, scooping crazily with her flippers. "Rory? Rory, where are you?"

She glanced over her shoulder—he was far away, making snowballs to protect Muriel.

Realizing that she had run out of ammo, the lion took advantage and leaped onto the roof of the den.

"Jump off, Muriel!" yelled Rory, hurling a snowball with all his might. It hit the lion right between the eyes.

"Bullseye, dude!" yelled Clive.

As the lion reeled backward, Muriel hopped down and raced toward Blue.

The lion clawed the air and growled. To be pelted by penguins was seriously humiliating. If the tigers ever found out, he'd never live it down. He would have to kill anyone who trespassed into his enclosure or he'd never be able to hold his head up again. Who should he go for first—the fairy penguins scrabbling near the railings, or that nice, plump rockhopper...?

"Rory, *look out!*" screamed Blue as the lion leaped off the roof and landed in front of him.

"Oh my cod, it's cornered him," said Muriel. "Dig faster, Bloop! *Hattyyyy! Brendaaaah!* Get down here and dig from the outside. Bring the boys!"

Rory couldn't go forward, and having backed away slowly, he found himself pressed up against a large rock. There was no escape to the left or right—his path was blocked by shrubs. Even worse, he had an audience. The two little girls were back, showing their grandparents where they'd dropped the toy penguins, and once Granny had spotted the real penguins in the wrong enclosure, the word had spread and a crowd soon gathered.

"Any last requests, fish-face?" snarled the lion as it unsheathed its claws.

"Erm... let me think... D-don't eat me?" stammered Rory.

The lion showed its sabre-sized teeth.

"Sorry, not an option. I can't let my public down. People have paid good money

147

to see a ferocious beast, not a pussycat. Prepare to die, bird."

Muriel put her flippers over Blue's eyes.

"Don't look, Bloop. It won't be a pretty sight. I know I tease you about Rory, but he is kind of cute and being eaten is so going to ruin his looks."

Blue pushed Muriel's flippers away and scanned the snowy enclosure.

"The toy chicks..." she said. "Where did I leave them?"

Muriel's feathery eyebrows shot up in the air.

"*What?* The chicks are *toys?* I've risked life and limb and ruined my feather-do for two *stuffed toys?*"

Blue spotted one of them over by the den.

"You and me both, Muriel."

Scooting on her belly across the snow, she grabbed the toy chick, and as the lion lunged at Rory, threw it at the back of the big cat's head.

The lion whisked around and mistook the fluffy, fabric chick for the real thing. It pounced and ripped it to shreds.

"Run, Rory!" she cried.

"Faster!" screeched Muriel.

They raced to the edge of the enclosure and, breathing in, squeezed through the bars and were pulled to safety by the rescue party waiting on the other side.

"Hooray!" cheered the crowd.

"Boo!" roared the lion.

But just when the penguins thought they were good to go, they walked straight into the zookeeper.

CHAPTER NINE

A Party of Penguins

The zookeeper stared at the huddle of penguins in astonishment. He took his glasses off and cleaned them, but there was no denying it—here were four fairy penguins and three rockhoppers on the loose.

"How the...?" he muttered, checking in his pockets to see if the key to their enclosure had been stolen. No, there it was, still attached to its chain.

Had he forgotten to lock their door at feeding time? He scratched his head. No, he'd definitely locked up; he remembered how hard it was to turn the key in the icy lock.

"How on earth...?" he exclaimed.

"Don't tell him, Rory," said Blue.

"Oh, like he can understand Penguin, Bloop," muttered Muriel.

The zookeeper pulled out his walkie-talkie and summoned help as the little girls' grandparents confronted him.

"Those poor penguins could have been eaten alive!" said Grandma.

"I hope you remember to lock up the lions," said Grandpa crossly. "If they eat my granddaughters, I shall want compensation."

"That mean old lion tore my chick dolly's head off!" roared one of the girls.

The zookeeper did his best to apologize, and having refunded their tickets out of his own pocket, gave the girls gift-shop vouchers to buy new chicks.

"Let's make a run for it while he's distracted," urged Rory. "If we scatter, he'll never catch us. We have to keep looking for the chicks."

Blue looked up at the heavy gray sky and frowned.

"Rory, it's sunset soon. We'll never find them in the dark and even if we did, how would we find our way back? Brenda wouldn't be able to read the signs."

Muriel put her foot down.

"It's too far and I'm not walking another step."

A zoo truck approached. Muriel held out a flipper as if to hail a cab and to the penguins' surprise, it pulled over and stopped right next to them.

"How did she *do* that, Brenda?" whispered Hatty.

Muriel struck what she thought was a glamorous pose.

"I am just *so* sophisticated," she cooed as the driver got out.

Unfortunately, she didn't look quite so sophisticated when he picked her up by the legs and flippers and carried her kicking and screaming into the truck.

"Unhand me, you big baboon! Mind my head feathers!"

"Like he can understand Penguin, Muriel," scoffed Blue as the zookeeper ushered her up the ramp into the back, along with Hatty, Brenda, and the boys.

"Cool!" said Eddie. "I've always wanted to ride in a truck. Let's sing a song, Clive."

"OK," said Clive, clearing his throat as the zookeeper jumped into the truck and pulled away. "Altogether now… Ten green bottle-nosed dolphins, hanging on a wall; ten green bottle-nosed dolphins hanging on the wall; and if one green bottle-nosed dolphin should accidentally fall..."

Muriel put her flippers over her ears.

"Oh my cod—*you'll* 'accidentally' fall in a minute! Why are we singing? The chicks are still missing."

The penguins went quiet for a moment; then Blue spoke up.

"You did something nice for once, Muriel. That's worth singing for."

Muriel thought for a second, then her beak split into a huge smile.

"I did, didn't I? I saved Rory from the lion, didn't I, Hatty? Didn't I save Rory, Brenda?"

Brenda and Hatty nodded vigorously. Even though it was Muriel's fault the girls had dropped the chicks in with the lion,

she hadn't done it deliberately. And she'd more than made up for it by jumping in to save her friends. Rory appreciated that more than anyone.

"Thanks, Muriel," he said.

Muriel wasn't used to being thanked, and her eyes went all sparkly.

"So brave," said Brenda.

"So fearless," added Hatty.

"Warren is *so* going to kiss me now! Let's *sing!*" insisted Muriel, brushing away a tear and conducting them with her flipper. "Let me hear you, Bloop! 'Nine green bottle-nosed dolphins hanging on the wall; nine green…'"

As the penguins sang their hearts out, the hippos heard them and joined in, even though they didn't really understand the lyrics.

"Hey, Doris. What's a dolphin when it's at home?"

"Who cares, Henry? Just sing... 'Eight green bottle-nosed...'"

As the truck drove past the chimpanzees, the apes picked up the melody and the giraffe lifted her head and hummed along.

"Seven green bottle-nosed dolphins..."

"Six green bottle-nosed dolphins..." chorused the meerkats.

As the truck continued on its way, all the animals joined in, from the elephants to the emus, to the echidnas, and the zoo was filled with tuneful grunts, barks, bellows, and squeaks. Even the reptiles,

who had no voices, caught the vibes and tapped with their toes.

As the song came to an end, so did the journey, but as the truck stopped by

the penguin enclosure, the mood became somber.

The emperor chicks were still missing. Big Paulie would have to be told... and

Rory would have to face the music.

The driver opened the back of the truck. Delighted to be home, the rescue party waddled down the ramp, but Rory held back.

"What shall I say to Paulie, Blue? Maybe I could tell him a heron snatched the chicks or an escaped gibbon stole them... What do you think?"

"Just tell the truth," she said. "Paulie will never forgive you if you tell him a lie."

Rory still refused to get out of the truck.

"What if there's an angry mob waiting for me?"

Blue took him by the flipper.

"Rory, you just stood up to a lion. You can handle a bunch of angry penguins.

Come on, let's get it over with."

As they shuffled in through the door, they heard an almighty roar, but it wasn't a lion this time—it was the other penguins welcoming them home. They had been waiting anxiously, and seeing their friends safe at last, made them all cheer. A rather emotional Waldo was the first to give Rory and Blue a hug.

"Darlings! Marvelous to see you! I thought you'd been caught by an eagle or transferred to another zoo or something equally frightful."

As Warren and Waldo gave him a hero's welcome, Rory forgot for a moment that he had bad news to share—until the brown bears reminded him.

"Uh-oh, Paulie's coming over," said Orson.

"*Somebody's* got some explaining to do!" added Ursie.

Rory's stomach lurched as the boss picked his way through the crowd toward him.

"Where the heck did you go?" screeched Paulie. "I've been out of my mind."

A hush fell over the penguins. Rory shuffled his feet, then plucking up all his courage, he confessed.

"I… um… have something to tell you. You know when I was babysitting?"

"Yeth," said a little voice. "What about it, Wory?"

"Why do you look tho thad, Wory?" said another little voice. "Did you mith uth?"

Rory did a double take.

"Teeny? *Tiny!*" he cried. "Have you been here all this time?"

The chicks looked at him as if he was crazy, then fell on their backs in the snow and kicked their chubby legs in the air.

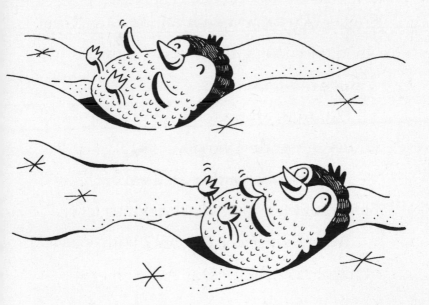

"Of courth we have, thilly! Where have *you* been?"

Rory was so shocked to see the emperor chicks, he didn't know whether to cuddle them or chase them.

"But…" he bumbled, "where did you go when I went snowboarding with—"

"You went… *snowboarding?*" exploded Big Paulie. "I trust you with my own flesh and blood and you play out in the snow?"

Rory hung his head.

"I know. It was wrong. I'm really sorry. I'll never, *ever* do it again."

"He tried *really* hard to get them back," said Blue. "In fact, he almost got eaten by a lion."

"Would have been eaten if I hadn't saved him," gloated Muriel.

Just then, Alaskadabra, the magician
emperor penguin, shuffled forward.

"Excuse me, Paulie. I have a feeling
this is all my fault."

He lifted up his belly. There, sitting on his exposed feet, was a newly hatched chick.

"The wife left me in charge," he said, "but baby Felicity wouldn't stop cheeping."

"Bad Felithity!" scolded Teeny.

Alaskadabra patted the hatchling's head and continued.

"When I saw the emperor chicks, I asked them to play with her at my place. I was hoping they would tire her out."

"He arthed uth to babythit like big chickth," said Tiny, "didn't you, Mithster Alathka?"

Alaskadabra nodded apologetically.

"I didn't mean to cause trouble. I simply asked the chicks if they could help my kid nap."

Orson, who had been listening in to the conversation as usual, turned to Ursie.

"Help my kid nap?" he said. "Ooohh! The way *we* heard it was 'Help me! Kidnap!'"

The rescue party glared up at the bears.

"Why do I ever listen to you?" yelled Rory. "You even told me you'd seen the kidnappers. *You almost got me killed!*"

"Don't yell at me," said Orson. "Ursie can't help it if he's hard of hearing."

"*Me?*" said Ursie. "That's rich coming from you, Cloth-ears!"

Big Paulie clapped his flippers together.

"Stop your bickering, bears—unless you want to end up as a rug. Rory, what you did was reckless and wrong. Even so, I admire your honesty and your bravery."

Rory bowed his head and promised never to let Paulie down again—and the great emperor penguin put a fatherly flipper round Rory's shoulder.

"Rory, Rory. We'll let bygones be bygones. We may not be the same breed, but as far as I'm concerned, you're family—you and Blue, Clive and Eddie, Hatty and Brenda… Yes, even you, my plucky little Muriel."

He turned to Alaskadabra.

"Conjure me up a hat, will you?"

The elderly magician fumbled about in his folds and patted his pockets. The big boss tapped his foot and whistled as he waited.

"Preferably today, Alaska…"

Finally he produced a red tissue-paper crown.

"Thank you," said Paulie. "And now, without further ado, I would like to celebrate the fact that my penguin family are home and safe."

Placing the hat on his head with great ceremony, he gave the order. "Let's party!"

Fresh snowflakes fell, and as the full moon rose like a disco ball, the penguins of City Zoo partied like it was Christmas.

THESE AWESOME ANIMALS
WERE BORN TO BE WILD!

Each book in the **Awesome Animals** series features the adventures of one spectacular species doing what animals do best . . . being wild! Their animal antics will keep you laughing out loud!

Each book, paperback, 176–192 pp., 5" x 7 3/4"
$6.99, NCR

Penguin Pandemonium
Can the penguins' performance save the zoo?
ISBN: 978-1-4380-0301-6

Raccoon Rampage
The gang prepares for their biggest heist ever!
ISBN: 978-1-4380-0302-3

Meerkat Madness
The meerkats discover something mysterious.
ISBN: 978-1-4380-0303-0

Panda Panic
Ping the panda has a plan to travel the world.
ISBN: 978-1-4380-0304-7

More Meerkat Madness
The kits go on a Kalahari adventure.
ISBN: 978-1-4380-0305-4

Penguin Pandemonium: The Rescue
Rory and his pals stage a daring rescue.
ISBN: 978-1-4380-0306-1

Merry Meerkat Madness
The meerkats learn all about Christmas.
ISBN: 978-1-4380-0307-8

Panda Panic: Running Wild
Hold on tight for Ping's biggest adventure yet!
ISBN: 978-1-4380-0308-5

COLLECT THEM ALL!

There are more
Awsome Animals at
www.barronsbooks.com/series/awesome
Win prizes, play games, and more!

Available at your local book store or visit **www.barronseduc.com**

Barron's Educational Series, Inc.
250 Wireless Blvd.
Hauppauge, N.Y. 11788
Order toll-free: 1-800-645-3476
Order by fax: 1-631-434-3217

Prices subject to change without notice.

In Canada:
Georgetown Book Warehouse
34 Armstrong Ave.
Georgetown, Ontario L7G 4R9
Canadian orders: 1-800-247-7160
Order by fax: 1-800-887-1594

(#284) R4/13

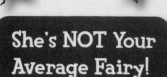